Fergus's Scary Night

For Jamie

First published in 2001 in Great Britain
This edition published 2015
Deepdene Lodge, Deepdene Avenue,
Dorking, Surrey, RH5 4AT, UK
www.bonnierpublishing.com

Text and illustrations copyright © Tony Maddox 2001

Printed and bound in China

ISBN: 978 1 84812 505 6 (paperback)

1 3 5 7 9 10 8 6 4 2

Fergus's
Scary Night

Fergus's
Scary Night

Tony Maddox

It was evening and the farmyard was quiet.
"Almost time for bed," thought Fergus.
Suddenly the pigs hurried by.
"Can't stop!" they oinked.

Fergus watched them go into the barn.
They were followed by the hens, then the ducks.
"I wonder what they're up to?" he muttered.
"I'd better take a look."

Inside the barn, the animals were huddled together
in front of the cow. She was telling them a story.
As she spoke their eyes grew bigger and bigger.
It was a ghost story!

"Humph!" growled Fergus.
"Silly ghost stories.
They don't scare me!"
And off he went to his kennel.

He was almost asleep when he heard
TAP, TAP, TAP on the kennel roof.
The fur stood up on his back.
"W-w-who's there?" he called out nervously.
"Just some big scary monsters!" came the reply.
Slowly Fergus peered outside and saw . . .

. . . the pigs laughing and dancing around.
"Were you scared, Fergus?" they oinked.
As they ran off, Fergus shouted,
"That wasn't very funny!"

Just then, the ducks rushed over.
"Help us, Fergus!" they quacked.
"There are skeletons in the vegetable patch.
We've heard their bones rattling."
Fergus groaned. When he went to look, he found . . .

. . . it was only a few plant pots
banging together in the wind.

On his way back to tell the ducks,
Fergus met the hens, shivering with fright.
"Look over there!" they whispered.
"It's a monster!"
Fergus turned and saw . . .

. . . just the shadow of some potato sacks
on the back of Farmer Bob's truck.
"Woof woof!" said Fergus wearily.
"Everyone back to bed."
Then they heard . . .

. . . the most horrible sound!
"Aaawwwaaaaahh! Aaawwwaaaahh!"
It was coming from the old shed
in the field behind the barn.
The animals crept closer.
They could see a light shining
under the doors.
"There's someone inside!"
whispered the hens.

Suddenly the doors flew open.
There in the lighted doorway
stood a dark and frightening shape.
"Aaawwwaaaahh!"
went the creature.
"Oooowwwaaaahhhh!"
went the animals, and
they turned and ran.

They rushed back into the
farmyard and into one of the sheds.
They crouched in the darkest
corner, not daring to breathe.
The shadow of the creature
came nearer, and nearer,
and nearer . . .

"Oh, hello!" said a familiar voice.
"What are you all doing out here?"
It was Farmer Bob.
"Hope my old bagpipes haven't kept you awake.
I'm a bit out of practice!"
"Humph!" muttered Fergus. "I knew there weren't
any ghosts or monsters on this farm."

Or were there . . . ?